The Story of
EASTER

Springtime in God's Family

A Coloring Book for Children

Text
Sr. Karen Cavanagh, CSJ.

Cover Illustration
Michael Letwenko

Text Illustrations
Edward Letwenko

MRP

REGINA PRESS
New York

The journey toward Easter begins on the first day of
Lent—Ash Wednesday. Christians receive ashes on their
foreheads. The priest says, "Turn away from sin and
believe the Good News."

During Lent God's family prepares for Easter. Special times are made to pray and to remember all that Jesus did for us. Prayer is an important part of Lent.

Doing without some favorite pleasures helps us to sacrifice during the days before Easter. Often Christians use what might have been spent to help poor people and hungry people.

Jesus, even more, wants us to reach out in service toward our sisters and brothers. We show our love in Lent when we take care of all God's family.

Jesus' teaching about prayer and love for even the least of God's children caused many to follow Him. He was honored by the people but He knew some would not accept Him.

Today we still remember this praise but we know it was followed by His suffering. On Palm Sunday we receive blessed palms and listen to the reading of Jesus' passion and death.

Jesus had come to Jerusalem to celebrate the Passover meal with His friends. He shared the first Eucharist with them and taught a very special lesson of service and caring.

Each Holy Thursday at the evening Eucharist the priest washes the feet of twelve people. Jesus said, "I have given you an example. What I have done you must do."

On Holy Thursday we are united with all God's family as we receive the holy oils which are used for the sacraments in our parish. The bishop blesses these at the Chrism Mass.

The Sacrament of fullness in God's family is the Eucharist. Jesus gave God's people this gift on the night before He would die. He wanted to stay with us forever.

He knew His time to suffer had come and Jesus was afraid. He did not want to die and He prayed God would take away the suffering. He felt so alone. He thought God and His friends had left Him.

Jesus' enemies wanted Him to die. He would die for His
message of love and caring for all people. His friends
were nowhere to be found. He began the journey
toward Calvary and death.

On a wooden cross the Lord and Savior of the world died for love of all of us. This wooden cross would become a "tree of salvation" bringing new life to all God's family.

Each Good Friday we remember Jesus' death on a cross. We gather as a family and honor the cross because our faith teaches that it truly is the "tree of salvation" which brings us new life.

ALLELUIA!

He has risen as He said He would. The death a
life that will last forever. Death is no longer an
This is the promise and message of Easter.

ALLELUIA!

ng of Jesus has won a new life for us. It is a
ut the beginning of a life that will last forever.

The promise and message of Easter is for all of God's family. Together we come to celebrate Jesus' journey which won life for all of us. All the earth sings for joy.

The promise of new life is celebrated with baptisms at Easter. At the Easter Vigil new members of the Christian family are baptized and receive a white robe symbolic of their new life in Christ.

Easter is a time of newness. We wear something new or special. We dress in our best as a reminder of our baptismal clothes and the new life we have in Christ.

At Easter Eucharist we are invited to renew the promises of our own baptism. We are blessed with holy water. The lighted candles are a sign we must be a light in the world.

On Easter morning children find gifts and surprises that celebrate new life. Easter baskets are filled with spring's green grass and the sweets and treats of new life.

One special Easter treat is colored eggs. They are decorated in rainbow colors—some are hand painted. Families paint flowers, crosses, bunnies and chicks on their eggs.

Chocolate crosses are adorned with candy flowers and beautiful butterflies. Because of Easter, the cross becomes a thing of beauty for God's family.

Chicks and rabbits are the new life of springtime. The butterfly tells again how new and beautiful life can come from a dark cocoon. The new life of Jesus came from darkness in a tomb.

Flowers are another Easter symbol. The beautiful and colorful flower blooms from seeds. The seeds must die in the ground so they can grow into a new life.

God has given us all this beauty in creation. All creation sings God's praise and reminds us of the care and respect it deserves.

The risen Jesus continued to walk this earth with His
friends. They did not always recognize Him but they
lived His message of service and love.

Sometimes we don't always recognize Jesus in the persons closest to us. Jesus promised to be with us whenever we gather to remember His life.

The life of the risen Jesus is ours to live. Our baptism calls us to be close to God, to be loving and caring for one another and to be ready to die to selfish ways.

All of us in God's family have been given this call. We are to live as Easter people and build God's family until Jesus comes again in glory. Alleluia!

Draw and color a favorite Easter picture...

WRITE YOUR STORY

_____

_____

_____

_____